To my wife Shana
Thank You!   fs

Written by Floyd Stokes
Copyright © 2008 by Floyd Stokes
Illustrated by Michelle Green
Graphic Design by Michelle Hassinger and Floyd Stokes
Translation by Tressimee R. Stokes, Mary Kratzer, Esmeralda Hectrick, and Hector Ortiz

First edition, 2012. All rights reserved.

ISBN 978-0-9797871-0-2

A publication of The American Literacy Corporation for Young Readers

Printed in China

¡Muy bien!

Camisa bonita

Gracias

Pantalones bonitos

Gracias

¿Me permites?

Claro

Gracias

De nada

Gracias

De nada

Gracias

De nada

¿Sándwich?

Sí, por favor

Es sabroso

Gracias

¡De nada!